A Black Bridge

T0097596

WESTERN LITERATURE SERIES

University of Nevada Press ▲▲ Reno & Las Vegas

A BLACK BRIDGE

Ralph Tejeda Wilson

POEMS

Western Literature Series

University of Nevada Press, Reno, Nevada 89557 USA

Copyright © 1982, 1983, 1984, 1985, 1986, 1989, 1992,

1993, 1994, 1995, 1996, 1997, 2001 by

Manufactured in the United States of America

Design by Carrie House

Library of Congress Cataloging-in-Publication Data

Wilson, Ralph Tejeda, 1955–

A black bridge : poems / Ralph Tejeda Wilson.

p. cm. — (Western literature series)

ISBN 0-87417-360-4 (alk. paper)

I. Title. II. Series.

PS3573.I46495 B57   2001

811'.6—dc21   00-011123

The paper used in this book meets the requirements of

American National Standard for Information Sciences—

Permanence of Paper for Printed Materials, ANSI

z39.48-1984. Binding materials were selected for

strength and durability.

FIRST PRINTING

10 09 08 07 06 05 04 03 02 01

5 4 3 2 1

For my parents,

Ralph Mervin Wilson and
Eugenia Amparo Tejeda Wilson

The world is but a bridge, build no house upon it.
The world lasts but an hour, spend it in devotion.
—AKBAR

As apparitional as sails that cross
Some page of figures to be filed away . . .
—HART CRANE

Contents

PART I THE HESITATION PITCH

Behind Grandfather's House, 3 | The Discovery
of Fire, 5 | The Hesitation Pitch, 7 | Dogfish, 9 |
Henzey's Pond, 11 | The Snowman, 12 | Like Love,
14 | The Fire Cat, 15 | Snowbound, 17

PART II A BLACK BRIDGE

A Black Bridge, 21 | Pearl Road Monologue, 22 |
Late at the *Dionysus*, 24 | Giving Blood, 25 |
Sleeping Dogs, 26 | The Nightmare, 27 | Fragments,
29 | Downriver, 30 | Leap or Become Invisible, 31

PART III THE GARDEN OF EDEN

Wheeling Pike, 37 | The Garden of Eden, 39 |
Runner with Turkey Vultures, 42 | Deep Kansas, 44 |
Cows with Windows, 46 | Carousel, 47 | Pastoral, 48 |
Walking on Water, 50 | Running the Dog, 52 |
Karl in Snow, 53 | In Praise of Beauticians, 54 |
Life and Art, 56

Acknowledgments, 57

THE HESITATION PITCH

PART I

Behind Grandfather's House

Out back was a black tarp
with snakes underneath it in summer
basking in moist grass and the steam
of compost. And just for fun,
the childish thrill, we'd lift an edge,
throw the dark curtain open to the sun
and watch the tangled mass wildly unravel,
go slithering out all around our feet.
Milksnakes, bullsnakes, garters:
harmless facsimiles in a Rockwell
version of paradise: my childhood:
the innocent, listless Sunday afternoons
spent at the grandfolks' waiting for dinner:
sauerkraut, pork, potatoes, and rhubarb pie.
Is it any wonder, having no pets
to torture, so much backyard wilderness
and actual time to kill, we would not
be drawn far through grapevines and appled
shade, always to that stinking pile of snakes?
What memory remains chaste
which had not once a touch of dread?
A grandfather requires a cough, his wife
stale gardenia perfume. For nostalgia's sake,
a sour-smelling house of kitsch
announced by a pair of flamingos
pinked upon the rolled front lawn.
The conversation should include arthritis,
Catawba wine, and for whichever sibling
still in reach, some repeated tale confirming,

even in youth, the oddness of your dad.
Everything, everyone you love,
must be flawed so perfectly
you can distill the momentary wealth
of that escape: closing the screen door softly
as the dishes are cleared and lamps are lit.
Their voices becoming the murmur
of cicadas' wings over the hushing grass,
as you stand at the foot of that darker plot,
waiting for someone to call you back.

The Discovery of Fire

In his father's oily garage, lit
only by a grimed window, Rodney Vick
tendered the secret he'd found squirreled away
of an entire box of Ohio Blue-Tips.
Unlike the magic offered in a comic's back pages—
X-ray glasses, jumping beans, Mr. Blackstone's
finger-sized guillotine—we were impressed
as he let us stroke the stick-dry stems,
brush with the whorled tip of an index
the sandy grain of the perched, pursed bulbs.
Each indigo egg, smaller than a fingernail,
with the edge of a fingernail he cracked one—
the scratch and splutter turned scintillant
down our spines, upfluttering
into a tame handheld wing.
                          Behind him
on the pegboard wall, the black gun
of an electric drill, various hammers,
slender grease-rinsed tools hung
in glinting declensions—our mouths
like those shiny o's—the rowed widening
apertures fluted of wrenches.
We knew it was wrong to touch
anything, how intimate and dangerous
the balanced instruments of adults,
how, if crazy Jerry Vick caught us
handy to that jimmied door,
there'd be hell to pay, the kind
Rodney wore in pale welts

memorized along his back and buttocks.
We didn't care. The air turned dusk,
a blue fume reeking of sulfur
as we played the trick on floor and wall,
on sawblade and shoe sole, on the teeth
tinily clenched of our prepubescent
zippers.
       The light was kindled
suddenly in our heads: the world
was combustible: its locks
could be picked, glintings stolen,
the sorry rest of it like tinder.
We filched all we could, bartering
futures of cigarettes, firecrackers, gasoline
against those charmed splinters slithered
like things alive preciously into our pockets.

Outside, grass blazed in the last light
of afternoon, the poplars turned
green wavering candles. From far off,
our parents were returning home,
remote in their customary orbits
threaded patiently toward day's decline,
the smoke already rising from their roofs.

The Hesitation Pitch

for Luis Tiant

Even my Mexican mother, having little use for *cubanos,*
loved him. Her private cheer: *U - G - L - Y, he ain't got no
    alibi!*
meant with affection. On the mound in Cleveland,
that black stump of a man with too-long arms
he could uncoil over the top, sidearm, or suddenly
    submarining:
leaving the hitters shaking their heads, staring, or bailing all
    the way out.
Through the dull factory grind of summer when the lake stank
of algae and Dow Chemical, the skyline fogged its curious shade
    of brown,
the Indians firmly, typically, in the cellar, he would be there
every fourth day like clockwork, warming up with his long
    underwear
showing, a golf ball of tobacco tucked in one cheek.
Back then, Detroit had Kaline, and Boston, Yastremski;
the Robinsons were in Baltimore: cities we knew as bad
as ours, but with teams that made them look better.
Better surely than Tiant in his first *Game of the Week* interview,
approaching the camera as if it might steal
his soul, magnifying instead the flat wedge of his nose and
    broken
English. It would be hard, but we would have to keep on waiting,
waiting as we had always waited, huddled in the collective memory
of Lou Boudreau and 1948, waiting finally for justice,
finally for Tiant on the bald hill of the mound,
serving up air: fastballs that rose or dropped by turns,
sliders, curves, the knuckler: whatever he concocted to do

the one job he was meant to do over and over again.
And we would be waiting for what Herb Score called
the *hesitation pitch,* that deliberately corkscrewed delivery
that turned him for a moment out toward center field
to face the vast wasteland of bleachers, the two-dollar seats
from where we could see him almost plainly hiding the ball,
sweating, sneering as he worked up the juice,
the whole time giving them his back.

Dogfish

Cleveland, 1969

In August when Erie was bad
with algae and heat, miles away
through a faucet you could still
taste it in your glass. And up close
along piers of jutting concrete
meant once for mooring barge
and ore boat, you could smell
what had come to school in shallows
shadowed beneath the docks.
Suckerfish, sand sharks, mudpuppies,
whichever you chose to call them,
hauled up and left with the hooks
still in them, lining the gangways
like rubbery slippers, like fleshy brown
galoshes collapsing in the sun.
When dogfish were landed,
no one threw them back, but fished
with the stench piled around them
as if to prove God-knows-what
was in them to do it, but the same
simple perversity. Staked out
under the sooted stacks of Republic
and Ford, you were raised
with mercury underneath the gills
of steelhead, with cankerous bass,
drank shots flaming in crude effigy
of the grim Cuyahoga. Shoulder to shoulder
with the unionized and unemployed

in pursuit of the sweet meat—perch
or walleye, the by-then-mythic lake trout—
what I remember best is the obstinance
of such crews, stooped in sunlight,
burnt-collared, pitching with curses
windward. And dogfish at the long end
of summer, lining the piers, working
their mouths, almost breathing
as you breathed then yourself
through teeth gritted down, swallowing,
staring out over the iron lake.

Henzey's Pond

memory, after Brueghel's *Hunters in the Snow*

Arch, ankle, the scintillant hiss and chatter
of blades whetted with midwinter sun
inscribing the smooth stone disc of the pond.
School figures, phonics worksheets, thumbed copies
of Baltimore catechism stashed inside
vinyl bookbags set out to mark the netless
posts of the goals. And the long bandaged sticks
like flattened bishop's crooks to slap hell
out of the nun-dark puck. No parents,
nor penguins afloat in their chaste whispering
raiment whipped faintly by loops of dangled
rosary beads. *Hail Mary! Dog-damn!*
Playing, in the heat of moments, at the edge
of blasphemy with hell's own bells, the childish
knockers of our tongues. Named for saints,
we wore them at our throats, sometimes knotting
the parochial tie embossed with Paraclete
like rude coronals around our heads
to appear more convincingly heathen.
Our pressed white shirts, moist and steaming
with sweat, were unbuttoned, unlaced
into billowing wings rising in the created wind
of our bodies as we raced across the sheening
glass outbrightened, without reflection.

The Snowman

If I had a son, I would go to his room
at bedtime and tuck him in. I would sit close
beside him and touch his hair and talk
of the long day, how night comes and we sleep

to be better for tomorrow. Or maybe we'd sit
in a chair by the window and look
at the sky, and I would point out the moon
and the North Star, and he would be tired

or too young to ask questions, and would not learn
that that is all I know of stars. And if it were
winter, and the house popped and creaked
as houses do, I would speak of what cold does

to the joints, how ground settles and wood
contracts with the ample arguments of air.
Or perhaps I'd pretend it was the snowman
we'd built, risen from the front yard, unable

to sleep with the family still awake, walking
on the roof to pass the time. How we might
keep him from our warm beds simply
by closing our eyes. And then I'd leave

the door open an inch from the jamb, so light
from my table might slip in to reassure him.
And as I go to my bed at night, the house creaks
and pops, and I lie awake and dream of how

I have no son, of how silent and still
the treetops are, the white roof, how my footprints
glow in ice behind me. The sky is beautiful
and full of stars. And it is cold and I am cold.

Like Love

The cat makes a nuisance
of affection—
how it is always waiting
among the familiar habits of home:
light steps to the doorway
where my approach sends it
in a soft curve around ankles,
mewing for attention.

The things it wants
are almost innocent:
ears rubbed, pink flesh
it can't reach caressed.
It wants to taste salt
on the flat of its tongue
and to feel sure fingers search
the slender links of its spine.

The lulling trill it makes
within its throat is like love
in return for food, water,
a body's warmth at night,
and even as I have seen before
pressed against a window
toward birds on a wire—
the slow involuntary movements
of its jaws are like love.

The Fire Cat

I

I have allowed for the yellow one, puniest
of the litter now gone: torn by cries
of dogs, coyotes, the squeals of tires
done with turning away from the inevitable.
I give it whatever I can, which is not enough—
the fat and skin, water in a tin cup.
The cat cowers beneath the porch all night
and will not come to be petted.

II

My wife tells me I am cruel in pretending
at providence and warns of what breeds
between necessity and indifference. She is right.
There is no telling what can come of something
held halfway to the heart, and I have heard it yowl
at night deep in its furred throat, heard it yowl
down there, somewhere beneath the floor,
and yowled myself, the gaped and guttural phrase
I could not touch with my tongue nor press
back into the cavity of my body.

III

On the rim of a rusted garbage can, the fire cat
bristles and slinks. Flames dance and ash smolders
in a crackling pile of chicken bones. Soon it is

dancing itself, nimble on the heated edge,
its yellow head weaving flame, ringed with smoke.
It knows what it is not to be touched, to keep
itself from that other burning. It snatches
what it can, and drops clear.

Snowbound

That day there were no roads
to travel between river and town:
all blanked out, markless
but for the sky coming down
in fragile, floating pieces.
I moved such stuff as I could
with a shovel meant
for a garden, and thought of her
stirring the froth of lentils
inside, how in another time
we might have kept to bed,
drunk whisky, and rooted
for such weather. In that drift
I stood, knee-deep in dross
while the cramped heart labored
where I bent over it, digging
against the numbness that slowly
took me. I was thinking of stories—
how the needle-bite of cold
becomes an easiness one mistakes
for warmth, falling into it
like sleep. The air was keener
than memory and my breath bloomed
within it, curiously visible,
as the blade sank so deep
I could not lift it. I left
it there. The snow fell.
The world became what it became.

A BLACK BRIDGE

PART II

A Black Bridge

Arcing over water, carrying rails
that zebra-striped the moon
and river, that black connection
between town and desert held
them: drifters, bikers, aging
hippies who camped in the flats
beneath its shadow and traded guns
for dogs, lovers for lovers, who gave up
good whisky for the sting of home
brew, drank mezcal and chewed
the worm, who sat, staggered,
strangled their fear with leather
talk, ate buttons of peyote
and stumbled into night, shaking
with strychnine and searching for God
in the cactus hills. And some who climbed
hand over hand, from nowhere
to nowhere, only to be closer
to what seemed a heaven, scaled
the framework of black horizon
and standing there saw how the tracks
stretched out in flat and fixed
directions, who looked below for faces
and found only shapes with voices distant
as the sound of water, who answered
to no one, but slipped between the ties
and dropped indifferently
into a counterfeit of stars.

Pearl Road Monologue

for Joey Conlan: 1955–1981

Joey, they've closed down the bowling alleys
again tonight, and in the last lit telephone
booth on Pearl Road, the receiver is still
missing. We've got no one to call anyway,
no dope, and the 7-Eleven won't be
selling beer until Monday. I figure you're thinking
we've been through this before. But to make it worse,
I can't find the words I scribbled down
on your bathroom floor, trying to work the acid
out of my blood. I'm telling you, I had it right
for awhile, remembering exactly as it was that August
night, drunk with work, with beer, on our asses
laughing at those dumb GI's breaking pool
cues across their khaki thighs. And oh it was fine,
the way we bought off the highway patrol
with our good looks, walking that straight line
with the best of them. This is a talent
I think I've lost since then, the kind of luck
that intimates immortality until the first
flashlight in your face that goes off
like a loaded gun.

      Joey, I'm still seeing stars
of angel dust and dreaming Las Vegas nights
where the girls glide by all kandy-kiss smiles
and mechanical arms are dropping their sweet
pocketfuls of God. This was your dream, I know,
but I've a need to get it right, so I can quit
clenching and unclenching like the fingers

in a mother's heart, damning and goddamning your sister,
my sister, that dilettante Cassandra and her faithless
boyfriend who fed you snow and easy talk
of money, and drove like hell out into the desert
night in a coke-panic of gunshots, leaving
you there with your whole life coming up
snake eyes.
        Joey, where do we go now
that the bowling alley is closed? I'm out
here on Pearl Road killing time, wishing
for a railroad yard to haunt, going back
in a one-eyed truck with so much empty
space to fill. It used to take until morning,
you on top of the stacks sending down
cases of number sixteen cans so fast
the conveyor belts would sing and shake.
And I'd catch them, every goddamn one,
with just enough sweat and swing
so the rhythm was there between us, the work
wet and easy. We never knew how easy,
clattering through boxcar nights where what we hauled
was just some simple weight, not the dead
stuff dreamed or remembered. I'm telling you,
I had it right for awhile, even your transparent
card-sharking grin. I know it doesn't matter.
Those words were just to keep me believing
it wasn't all a lot of lost motion,
and all of this, just a lot of talk.

Late at the *Dionysus*

In this whisky light we are sating
appetites too common to name.
This woman who does not feign
timidity, but makes a slow show
of bravado, knows it. The black
red-eyed bartender knows it, and
the dark-suited gentlemen in the front
row. Here, hunger becomes a dance
for the openhearted, undulating
with bared belly and stacked on high
stiletto heels. Intentionally baroque,
its flourishes are designed
to delay revelation, its music
to mark the time. Think of this, then,
as inspired choreography, a cakewalk
between cock and grave. Consider art
a loosening of scarves, a swaying
ass, a cradle of hips and thighs.
Imagine precisions deftly paraded,
the wink proffered behind gauze.
So much ripeness, this sincere applause.

Giving Blood

No, it doesn't hurt, does it?
Not the cold orange unguent daubed
on the vein, nor the sly incision
of the needle, nor the airy tingle
of webs silked between the fingers.

All that prefaced mere unease
is draining away into something
like peace, the paleness of the left hand
which does not understand, but like a stunned
fish in gelid water thicks with slow fins.

No, it doesn't hurt: neither languor
nor the bald spot spreading inside the head
as you watch the flaccid bladder fill:
a dark, updangled moon
from which you somehow expected

more light: the ambering sluice
of one's self made luminous,
its treacle comported as diadem,
its leavening a burnished dusk.
No, it doesn't hurt,

though there is some sinking sense
of separation: the body's ink
betraying a doubt made flesh:
lifting your eyes as the arm is folded
like a wing back over the breast.

Sleeping Dogs

Again tonight, my neighbor's blue hound
is baying, all throat,
as if she might swallow
the moon, or keep it, treed
in the sycamore it has climbed.
Far off, her complaint
has become familiar, echoing
over yards and houses to others
tethered in their small circles.
Even now, I can feel them
moving, tightening
against the loops of cages
and pawing the cold ground
for whatever is there, just as I,
who have been worrying
this same spot, sprawled
under the headboard and knotted
linen, am looking for a way out
of consciousness: the slow downward drift
of stars and snow, the moon
a white bone of light hung
in the window like an empty cup.
And the hound's lone lingering vowel
following, filling
up nothing, nothing
over the dreamed earth.

The Nightmare

begins with a voice at the end of a line:
a voice that rings and enters out of a time

you kept in your sleep. You wake now and it breathes
of nothing familiar. It breathes

with difficulty into your ear where once
it whispered, moistened your cheek with its nonsense.

The voice can say nothing of love. What it speaks
of is ruin, of how hollow it is, weak,

how it won't ever recover. The voice goes on
like this, vainly, for a great while. It goes on

and finally you realize that it blames you
for everything. And, in fact, it is true:

you *are* to blame for everything. You would like
to hang up now. You would like to forget your life,

but the voice has memorized it completely.
It has gone through a lot of trouble to be

this honest, and wants you to hold up your end.
The voice is telling a story it contends

will happen in a very short while. It wants
you to be lucky and first to take account.

The voice says it will soon stop talking, that words
mean nothing anyway, and that afterwards

it expects to be missed.

Fragments

all afternoon up the survey road
the city   over my shoulder
     dwindled   vertical turn and
deer trail then   steaming spoor
and split-hoof tracks   step by step
into thinning air   the fragments
clarified   purple threads of fire-thorn
   maples flaming far down the gorge
and beneath rock outcropped
            like a bird's beak
where I bent for the scrub oak's
   spill   of acorns, waxy
feel of them in my hand   I found the
bleached and hollow wheels
   of snail shells
in numbers   inexplicable
their small mouthfuls of dirt

Downriver

In morning without a proper light
we float black water spreading
into fish-belly silver. Distant
gulls wheel out of dreams of coffee
cups, brackish ale. Stars
trickle out of sight. A pinhole
opens in the sky, drawing yolk through
the firmament of an egg. Some birth
awaiting a reciprocal motion. The line
tugs in my hand and I haul the hook
against the weight of a worm
grown spectacular. *Play it, you've got
to play it,* the old man says. No luck.
The river laughs. *Follow the loons,*
the old man cries. *Expert fishermen.*
All of us spiders at the oars. They
cry and are never there to see them.
We toss toward circles, bubbles,
whatever's underneath. We snag
trees, each other, the old man himself.
Patience, he advises, *and a steady hand.*
We wait. Day passes. It is night
and we leave all lines drifting. In morning
we pull out a drowned bird, a loon
with a hooked grin. We cut
the trout out of its belly.

Leap or Become Invisible

for James O'Ryan and Kevin Cantwell

Humping upridge most of morning, hunting
for water, a pocket so blue it would taste of sky
and May ice and rainbows firm to the hook,
flashing alive at the ends of your fingers.
We walked too damn far for nothing we found
but that glorified watershed shimmering
in saddle-backed sun. One trout, and I didn't
even catch or kill him right.
                              Dear James,
sometimes the world is beautiful and won't give
you what you want. I pulled him out, I swear,
by accident, hooked so deep the gills pumped
blood in my hand. I gutted him clean and saw then
that he was still breathing. I didn't know
what I was doing, and it doesn't help.
                              Somewhere
over the peaks of the Wasatch, perhaps
while you were being born, coming down
that ridge where deer trail turned tail-blind
into granite, Kevin said, *Who knows? Maybe they leap*
or just become invisible. We were looking
for the way out, and so were you, as we sounded
toward the purl and rush beneath us, stream-fed
and sweating with labor, until a violet pool
bloomed.
                How can I say what swam through the locked
valves of my heart, wall-eyed, tongueless for air,
where I hunkered down over the bruise-bright surface
of the water? I waited and waited, and every now and then

lifted the line in my hand, its single hook centered
through the orange salmon's egg to remind me
of the absurdity, thinking of the flushed ripeness
of a woman I knew well enough, of her saying
it probably wasn't mine, anyway.
                                    To be properly lost
is a gift of nature, the way deer take these high trails
in stride, as we pick through scrub oak and sage
and the balled roots of maples to find them
gone, their halved tracks like arrows pointing
the way, no way you could follow. The seeker
who has held them between wedged sights
and touched the cold steel to life knows
killing is a kind of possession. Your good parents
someday will have to let you go, alive
into the stricken world as if to mock
their tenderness, their love unbound, fleeing
upon steeper paths than these.
                                    From the blue edge
of water, I entered as shadow and held myself
stone-still, my length cast, deepening where it dropped clear
down to the bottom. I cannot say what mastered
the weight that floated there, its wishbone yoked
around the sudden gold barb in its throat. I reeled
and its body flashed, spectral between worlds, closing,
opening unto the left-handed loom, the rod suspended
in disbelief.

So grace is just as unlikely, or comes
unbidden to lie in the sun with glazed, unearthly eyes.
So I knelt over the fleshed glitter, cold with light
shuddering under my hands, and undid what was left
to do. This, like pity, a gift for taking, as if
through acts committed in error we could reenter
worlds broken by our making.

Leap or become invisible,
Kevin said, and in abstract I thought of you come
bawling, swaddled in the blood of your mother.
And of the other who dropped unbidden, unanswered,
whose form is the absence and imagined beauty
of deer fleeing, of the shattered arc to light
of a trout struck full-bodied in its hunger,
of the unblemished opal surface
of water into which doubt is cast.

Dear James,
trust nothing I tell you too completely.
Sleep until you are ready. Time savors.
Time takes to set things right.

THE GARDEN OF EDEN

PART III

Wheeling Pike

Through the windshield, the slow day would unfold
along highways tarred between one-horse towns,
past birch hollows and hickory groves, under chestnut
leaves sometimes hung so low, I'd slow the truck,
hear their green palms slapping upon the roof.
And hills set between narrow poplar rows
so precipitously inclined toward sun,
I'd gear down, shade my eyes, feel the cab rise
almost weightless out of one long valley
toward the brink of the next, afloat in the high seat.
And I remember the whistle-stops run
by Mom & Pop, pale girls in IGA's
snacking on Moonpie and RC cola,
the tight fit of their eyes on a pressed shirt,
a new face, the shiny machine outside,
afraid, sometimes, to talk, to count out loud,
to mistake any part of their daydream.
And towns of soot not even the river
could wash clean, coal cars linked in grudging
stream through landscape cut away, black bedrock
swarmed with yellow dozers, spindly backhoes,
the great-mandibled mechanic shovels
behemoth across the water, feeding
on earth, air, vista of company housing,
stacks and store, one hotel, two bars,
and a Baptist church without a steeple.
And down the road finally toward Wheeling,
toward sunset where the river widened,
if you were lonely or just listening,

the cb filled, channel by channel,
with the chatter of strangers sporting
flamboyant or oddly affecting names,
the least of which might be *Lonely Beaver*
followed by directions as to where to stop.
And I remember a Holiday Inn
with a gin joint downstairs, the doorway framed
and fitted with the front of a Mack truck,
a hinged grille so you could swing right in.
Thursday nights, Bobby Del and Bobby Sue
played country. A brother and sister, twins.
Him, blind. Her, pretty as you ever saw.

The Garden of Eden

It's hard to believe you can get there
so easily. But the signs begin
on I-70 west of Salina, and Route 232
is a paved road. You couldn't miss it
if you tried, once past Wilson's dammed
and shallow lake, heading into Lucas
where stop signs bob like apples
in sunstroke heat. There are arrows
everywhere.
           It occurs off a side street
being steamrolled and oiled by a man
who looks like Lazarus in a Massey-Ferguson
ballcap. He waves. You think of Charon floating
his barge down a tarred river.
                It happens as it could
in any neighborhood, small town or suburb,
where the familiar house on the corner
has suddenly sprouted into a jungle-gym
of the grotesque: cement rising out of the dust-choked
yard into a semblance of trees, a scaffolding
for a 3-D picture book in which Cain
is fleeing and Abel lies stone-dead
only a moment after the crime.
There is, of course, a serpent
which winds its way in hanging mortar
through scenes more obscure: a Confederate
priming his musket over a pile of bones:
a jackal rising on two legs, panting

toward the tree-dangled fruit, his testicles
protruding too obviously.
                              The man was a carpenter,
old Dinsmoor, and eighty-two when he fathered a child
to a twenty-year-old wife just to prove
that the doctors hadn't read their Bibles.
Then this place began.
                              I'm sure there were problems.
It's hard not to reinvent the story of Noah
in the faces of his neighbors as, in the beginning,
they peered through windows and trimmed their lawns
with a curious and concerned intimacy, before paying
the two bits required for a gander inside.
What they found was not unlike their own:
a parlor and kitchen, two bedrooms and the one
he died in, his clothes still hanging behind the door,
the gray silk vest he kept for show, stained with spittle
from his own tobacco. A man before his time,
some must have said, most probably shaking
their heads and wondering how best to keep
the kids away.
                              Out in back, where we walk
now, beneath such works as *The Crucifixion
of Labor* and the statue of abstract *Liberty*
plunging a spear into the head of a snake,
we might imagine this as the arbor
where his young wife walked. Perhaps there,
where stands his mausoleum, inside it a glass

case and open coffin where we can indisputably see him
gone to rot, perhaps there she kept a garden
once herself. There is no invention that can aid us
to enter her mind as she tends that plot
in the hot Kansas sun, a hundred miles of nowhere,
an eternity, surrounding her on every side.

But see now

how she is bending to her own garden
and as he calls she is rising with dirt
still upon her knees. She hurries toward the porch
because the steps are stone and his eyes
cataracted, and so she must take them
briskly and by hitching her skirt, dropping
what she has gathered for her children
in that short, emphatic flight.

Thus,

he finds her: flushed and breathless before him,
perfected by her trembling and riper than any
object that could fall, giftlike, into his startled
human hands, while above, some bust of an angel
continues to point its outraged and comical finger.

Runner with Turkey Vultures

Here, you don't have to lie
down or die to get noticed:
only break stride, stumble,
push harder than what's intended
to find yourself knee-deep
in your own body.

Here, mortality rises
with you out of dust
and sweat, out of gravel
caught in your skin and breath
you can't keep in your lungs,
lifting over the tops of cottonwoods
dark as the taste of blood.

What's necessary is a way
of believing in distance:
in the road beneath your feet
and wherever you've already been
without the trouble of this horizon
or these shadows pressing
into the mind's soft wax.

What's needed is a way
of coming to yourself
alone in the glare of noonday grass,
of finding that it is always

yourself circling in familiar flesh,
that the road goes on,
casual and changeless,
and is never the way home.

Deep Kansas

Ah, that country, how it seemed all a horizon
that the wind, constantly, was trying to fill.
Its long undulance of grasses, steady strumming
of wires stretched post-to-post, its pale-dirt roads
going nowhere, sinking or rising through clouds of
dust.

And often, in the ploughed yet unplanted field
behind the hermitage of abandoned farmhouse,
or at the intersection of bare and unmarked
country lanes, how in the midst of that empty cross
or fallow land, the wind seemed almost to grow

confused, or, intimately, somehow profane—
turning inward with lifted earth upon itself,
spiring upwards toward form or perhaps direction
in a semblance both of pillar and fountain,
which was violent, beautiful and momentary.

Dust devil, boll weevil, the ache at the heart
of the vegetative heart mown by the coming
of spirit. I think of the gold corridors
of wheat which once I had walked, heavily,
with a burlap bag dragged over my shoulders.

Of maize, the silvery reminiscence
of schoolgirls in its locks. And rows of sunflowers
imperceptibly adjusting their glance

like the happy-faces of little stoic priests
slowly dropping their seed-teeth, one-by-one.

And the wind, where was it in those torpid days
between labor and harvest, while the nameless worm
ate and spun its shroud over the withered anthers?
Somewhere, as I imagined then, down the road.
Somewhere sifting the dust of that horizon.

Cows with Windows

Kansas State Experimental Farm

As an abstraction, I suppose there is
some need to know what goes on inside
them, a desire from which they themselves
are removed. Or so one posits, observing
their feckless saunter across phrenic grass,
food for thought amid the green profusion
of particulars growing toward sunset
indistinctly gold. Valed, vague, negative
in their capability to matter,
they suggest of their durance the idols
of a quaint preternatural belief
whose totems are attended by hierophants,
masked in their approach, vestured in white coats.
But here is no tinkling of bells, no flute
nor solemn drum—no coronals of blossom
garlanding the throat or crowning the brow.
Though one, laying his palm atop the flat
warm stone of the bovine skull, murmurs
in comforting Greek *Whoa* and *Whoa*,
as the other, with gloved fingers tracing
the gently heaving lyre of the ribs,
lifts the portholed window and reaches in.

Carousel

—after Rilke

The great, untrustworthy horses of wood
will not be broken, will not bow, nor bend
their heads to take sugar from a child's hand.
Suffering children, they remain composed,
heedless in their bearings of fashioned leap
or whirl, even of their own strange escape.

Beneath their tamping hooves, such painted grass
reflects the common green deemed of pasture,
the poled-up roof upon its axis turned
no less a sky lit by a ring of brass
for these, as they have always been creatures
of artifice, suited to their natures.

So in spin, this orderly revolve
in which they rise and sink again from view,
the winding calliope's chorded mews
and an occasional queer balloon waved
loose, wandered with awkward silken tether
beyond bounds, where volition seems error.

But the horses, constant, fixed in their traces
or saddled with small, amazed, frail riders,
plunge on through the wheel, breathlessly bridled
in postures whose each gesture effaces
wooden fact, flexed, turned by the hawker's heel
upon other courses, toward deeper fields.

Pastoral

for T. C.

It was grass that held the blue sky up,
the level green of a diamond unrolled
toward mountains still capped with snow.
And he, who I remember then, easily
shagging flies, stroking the ball flat
through the scything arc of the bat,
would joke, feeling the prowess of his limbs,
the season in its coming, of the boy, as he
had once been his father's, needing to learn
the game, the glove, how to keep his head down
on the short ones hopped through the dirt.
He disappeared midsummer, and I did not hear
how his child had died until sometime thereafter.
Unaccountably, as it was told, called by
some name, a euphemism, *failure to thrive*.
I saw him once after that, lingering late
over lettuce and melons in a fluorescent grocery,
maintaining in the wide, too-well-lighted aisle
the look of a man abstracted from himself,
graying and thinner, his eyes as if glassing
toward some scene bent always over his shoulder.
This season, my own, and I had not thought
of him at all until these past few weeks,
waking with a child who fed and slept
not well or enough. Oh, nothing so serious
sensible care could not cure, though in the dark
we learn to doubt sometimes without distinction.
I had not considered him for many years,

though as I waited and watched and walked
the soundless nursery floor, I carried
the thought of his small son in my arms.

Walking on Water

My father swam oceans
in my childhood: from Atlantic
to Pacific, across cold northern lakes.
He held us in his arms
and tossed us to that water
that we might learn to move as he:
buoyant and easy, taking breath
between the swells. Hard December
now and Erie is choked
with ice where the highway bends
to bear me homeward, thinking of how
I would like to come back to him
out of something proven, an event
more considerable than this life
I wear, comfortable as a coat.
I would like to come back across this lake,
just as it is, the way I'd heard
of Canadians crossing miles of silver
and clambering its frozen hulls
up into the harbor. I would go as long
as it took, following my shadow,
some shadow, in the hard pale haze.
Through the slits of my eyes, wet
with wind, I would see him trudging
the slush again, black-booted and severe
as the day of the March breakup
when ice buckled and opened between us
and shore, and ten fishermen and I
trailed his jagged horizontal

all the way home. I would like to come back
better than I did that day, numb
and cursing, stung always by the cold
heroics of a man I could not comprehend:
his poverty, his war, the bulldog
on his forearm blued in perpetual glare
against armies incontrovertible
as time. The years flood back now,
a gulf deep enough to drown in
without will or anger or the steadfast
strokes of love, and I cross it,
relearning the lesson of my father
who taught me how to walk on water.

Running the Dog

More walking really, because I was tired
and the dog took my lead, straying
left and right, but near always
the sound of my voice on the path we kept
away from fishermen casting their hooks
and sinkers of lead into the brown splash
of river, away from the town's
banked edge, where the tongues of bells
emptied themselves upon the water.
We crossed a ridge into trees
where the path became a wrinkle
and the dog shouldered blindly
through sawgrass, and I, with arms raised
to avoid the itch of those needles
saw how the dogwoods had been shattered
by the night's storm and earth opened
around roots, naked and nervelike
in the sun. And going back another way,
there was a field, level and sweet
with goldenrod and thick with the hum
of bees. It was like wading
a promise of honey, all that color,
or maybe like thinking of God, not
an intelligence, but beauty dominating
what had been there the whole
hot afternoon. We paused,
choosing our way through, and then we ran.

Karl in Snow

Overcome with an admittedly *bourgeois* desire
for pleasure, he pulls on his coat, walks out
onto the backyard patio for a smoke.
On the corrugated tin awning above him,
a ticking, not unlike the linear expression
of time, condescends as snow—
a history which accumulates, deepening in erasure
over the cobbled walk, pathways worn through grass.
Silently in the Christian night, he gathers
a garden back to mind—fat phalluses
of cucumber and comic zucchini splayed
beneath swayed, feminine fronds.
Green beans, onions, basil. Acrid rue.
And the climb, which Mendel is yet to consider,
of sweet peas upon their wires. Mown, and cold,
labor resolves itself, from the laborer's point of view,
into a *tabula rasa*—a locale where will
is nullified, or perhaps can be rewritten?
Two trees stand off to one side. Pear and willow.
One fruitful, the other mere ornament: articulating
in their upheld limbs the darker, finer lines
of a dialectic. He empties the ash from his pipe
into the frosted bowl of birdbath, and observes
how, almost *metaphysically*, a term he rejects,
the snow balances atop each singular slat
of the picket fence like tiny Russian tiaras.
He brushes his boots at the door, and goes back in.

In Praise of Beauticians

It is easy enough to criticize—
to speak of sincerities which fall short,
of styles whose confections
seem laughable, of embellishments
whose blushes do not deceive.

So tonight, I want to say something kind
for all the beauticians whose hands are stained,
whose feet are tired, whose work,
saith the preacher, is vanity.
I want to say that desire

is better than the sight of the eyes
in most cases. That the mirrors are glass.
That time is a comb with teeth
and Death the customer in the chair
no one ever satisfies.

I want to offer the perishable fruit
of my lips, the homely worm of my tongue
in praise of beauticians
whose province is the ordinary
pale of patience and mercy.

I want to imagine the palpable
dusk of their fingers, the painless shearing
and fallen floss like wool
deepened into cloud beneath their feet.
I want to resign my crown,

my follicled flesh to the tapering
wings of scissors, to the dark delicate
wands penciling a wry
Hellenic arch above each closed eye
which is the tracing in ash

of an irony in likeness to ourselves.
Because our moment in the sun passes
into convincing shade,
and silvery as reminiscence
the luster which thins our days,

let us wring from mouth's faintly mocking bell
mugged across a wilderness of glass,
smile's bitter ornament
opened like a paying hand, in praise
becoming of beauticians.

Life and Art

The alligators at Parrot Jungle
weren't much. They never moved
a muzzy muscle, covered with shit
as they lay on the rocks, gloating
with fat almond eyes, and my brother
Jeff spat a hawker right on one
which didn't twitch or blink
to signify he was even alive or
existed much or that there were really
orchids and bananas in the tropics
or slashes of sunlight searing green
cords of bamboo, and the flamingos
were beautiful and bright as roses
or a dream maybe of effeminate military
men marching on hipless pink legs
across the emerald lawn, pretending
every now and then as they minced
and spread the dark undersides of wings
that they might fly off or ripple
the silver glass of water or maybe
even copulate, while the alligators
sipped mud and stank and ate up
those pink bodies with their eyes.

Acknowledgments

Grateful acknowledgment to the editors of the magazines in which these poems, some in altered versions, first appeared:

Pendragon 1, no. 3 (Spring 1982), "The Fire Cat"; *Mid-American Review* 2, no. 1 (Fall 1991), "Runner with Turkey Vultures"; *Kansas Quarterly* 15, no. 4 (Fall 1983), "A Black Bridge," "Downriver," "Life and Art"; *New England Review and Bread Loaf* Quarterly 6, no. 2 (Winter 1983), "The Snowman," "Pearl Road Monologue"; *American Literary Review* (Spring 1994), "Carousel"; *Chariton Review* 10, no. 2 (Fall 1984), "Snowbound"; *Georgia Review* 34, no. 2 (Fall 1985), "The Garden of Eden"; *Three Rivers Poetry Review* nos. 27/28 (1986), "The Hesitation Pitch," "Running the Dog"; *Passages North* (Winter 1989), "Sleeping Dogs"; *The Journal* (Ohio State University) 16, no. 2 (Fall/Winter 1992), "Cows with Windows," "Deep Kansas"; *Puerto del Sol* (Summer 1993), "Behind Grandfather's House"; *Midwest Quarterly* (Summer 1994), "Fragments"; *Black Fly Review* 16 (May 1995), "Like Love"; *Seneca Review* 15, no. 2 (Fall 1995), "Leap or Become Invisible," "Karl in Snow," "Like Love"; *Poetry: USA* (October 1995), "Walking on Water"; *Cincinnati Poetry Review* 27 (Fall/Winter 1995), "Dogfish," "Henzey's Pond"; *Quarterly West* no. 19 (Spring 1985), "The Nightmare"; no. 42 (Spring 1996), "The Discovery of Fire," "In Praise of Beauticians"; *Jeopardy* 23 (Spring 1997), "Wheeling Pike," "Pastoral"; *Laurel Review* 31, no. 2 (Summer 1997), "Late at the *Dionysus*"; and *Willow Springs* (Winter 1997), "Giving Blood."

The author also wishes to thank his teachers for their patience, encouragement, and expertise, foremost among them Jonathan Holden, Larry Levis, Jacqueline Osherow, and Mark Strand.

Thanks also to Katharine Coles, Claudia Keelan, and Trudy McMurrin for their generosity and support of this manuscript.

And special thanks to Scott Cairns for his friendship, insight, and authenticity through the years.